Three Little Birds

by Lysa Mullady

illustrated by Kyle Reed

Magination Press • Washington, DC
American Psychological Association

For my mom, a loving soul who taught me the importance of being kind. Thank you for always believing in me —LM

To Mrs. White, who started all of this —KR

American Psychological Association
750 First Street NE
Washington, DC 20002

Magination Press is a registered trademark of the American Psychological Association.
Order books here: www.apa.org/pubs/magination or 1-800-374-2721

Book design by Sandra Kimbell
Printed by Worzalla, Stevens Point, WI

Library of Congress Cataloging-in-Publication Data

Names: Mullady, Lysa, author. | Reed, Kyle, illustrator.
Title: Three little birds / by Lysa Mullady ; illustrated by Kyle Reed.
Description: Washington, DC : Magination Press, an imprint of the American Psychological
Association, [2019] | Summary: Blue is upset when Red and Yellow go to find worms without him,
but feels even worse after starting a rumor that Red and Yellow are not getting along.
Identifiers: LCCN 2018008721| ISBN 9781433829475 (hardcover) | ISBN 1433829479 (hardcover)
Subjects: | CYAC: Gossip—Fiction. | Honesty—Fiction. | Birds—Fiction.
Classification: LCC PZ7.1.M8214 Thr 2019 | DDC [E]—dc23 LC record available at
https://lccn.loc.gov/2018008721

Manufactured in the United States of America
10 9 8 7 6 5 4 3 2 1

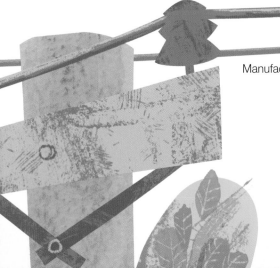

Three little birds, sitting on a wire, chirping about the day.

Red asked Yellow, "Do you want to go find some worms?"

Yellow replied, "Why not?"

Off they flew to find their snack, leaving Blue behind.

One little bird, sitting on a wire, feeling all alone.
"That's not fair! They didn't ask me to go!"
His mood turned dark and foul.

Along came two more little birds.
Green and Violet joined Blue.

Three little birds, sitting on a wire, chirping about the day.
Blue still felt hurt that Red hadn't invited him along.

Impulsively, he blurted out, "I heard Red say to Yellow that Yellow was the worst at finding worms."

Blue knew it was a lie.
But he thought: *Red deserves it for being mean to me.*

Green and Violet looked at each other in surprise.
Green asked Violet, "Didn't we just see Red and Yellow?"

"We **did**," replied Violet.

Green asked, "Do you think they are fighting?"

"Maybe," said Violet. Violet was a bird of few words.

Feeling curious, Green said, "Let's go see!"

Blue felt guilty for what he had done.
He said something that was not true, and now it had
started a rumor.

He wanted to take back what he said.
He opened his beak to speak, but the words didn't come
out fast enough.

Green and Violet were already on
their way, in search of the angry birds.
Once again, Blue was left behind.

Flying in the sky, Green spied Orange fluttering in a bath.
Green said, "Did you hear the news? Red hurt Yellow's feelings.
They're not getting along!"

Orange looked puzzled. "That's funny, I just saw them fly by.
They didn't seem upset at all."

"I know for a fact they are **fighting**," Green answered confidently. "Blue told me."

Orange decided to tag along to find out what the fuss was all about.

Violet saw Pink playing in a puddle.
Violet stopped to share the news.

"Feud!" was all Violet said.

"Where?" asked Pink.

"Come!" answered Violet, and flew away.
Pink quickly followed.

Green, Violet, Orange, and Pink all flew
together in search of Red and Yellow,
flapping furiously to find the bickering birds.

Meanwhile, Red and Yellow were scurrying around a field, happily finding worms.

With great gusto, the others landed around them.

"Fight!" yelled Violet.

Red and Yellow looked up.

"Fight? What fight?" asked Red.

"We heard you and Yellow were **fighting**," answered Green.

Red looked at Yellow.
Yellow looked at Red.
They shook their heads in confusion.

"We are simply looking for worms," said Yellow.
"We're getting along just fine."

Red looked at the group and asked,
"Who told you we were **fighting**?"

Pink said, "I heard it from Violet."

Orange said, "I heard it from Green."

Violet said, "I heard it from Blue."

Green said, "I heard it from Blue, too!"

Red said, "What you heard was not true."
He turned to Yellow and said, "Let's go talk to Blue."
Red and Yellow flew off.

The cluster of birds took flight,
following Red and Yellow in search of Blue.

Seven little birds, sitting on a wire.
There was no chirping at all.
Each one sat quietly, waiting to see what would happen next.

Blue was the most nervous of all.

"What did you tell Green and Violet?" demanded Red.

Timidly, Blue answered, "I said that you were hunting for worms."

Another lie.
Ashamed, he hung his head low.

Green challenged Blue. "That's not what you said!"

All eyes turned to Blue, waiting to hear his reply. Blue knew it was time to tell the truth.

"I did tell a lie. I said you told Yellow she was the worst at finding worms. But I never said you were **fighting**. I think Green made that up."

Green exclaimed, "What! That wasn't true?
I just assumed you meant they were **fighting**.
Didn't you **think** they were **fighting**, Violet?"

Violet agreed, "Yup."

Red was angry.

He didn't like when people said things that weren't true.
He wanted to scream at Blue.
He imagined yelling at the top of his lungs, *That's not fair!*

Instead, Red took a long, deep breath.
He knew how important it was to be calm and talk things out.
Even if Blue was wrong, Red still needed to do the right thing.

"What made you say that?" he asked Blue.

Embarrassed, Blue replied, "When you went with Yellow,
I felt left out. I was upset you didn't ask me to go."

Red realized he was wrong not to have included Blue.
"Blue, I'm sorry I didn't think to ask you to come along."

"That's alright, Red. I know you didn't mean to hurt my feelings. I was
just upset. But I was wrong to lie and make up that story. I'm sorry."

"Thanks, Blue. Next time, just ask to come along!"

Seven little birds, sitting on a wire, chirping about the day. Agreeing the world is a better place when words are used for kindness.

Never again did they lie or gossip. When hurt feelings occurred, as hurt feelings always do, they talked it out.

Seven little birds, sitting on a wire, enjoying the happiness friendship brings.

Note to Parents, Caregivers, & Professionals

Hurt feelings happen. There's no way to avoid it. It is natural to get angry when someone upsets us, and even common to want to seek revenge. Yet dealing with conflict in a spiteful way will result in the problem getting bigger; our goal should be peaceful resolution, not negative actions. Proactive problem-solving skills help kids get along and work together. We cannot erase conflict from our lives, but we can give our children the tools to deal with difficult situations.

How This Book Can Help

The story begins with Red unknowingly offending Blue. This results in Blue feeling upset and left out. Blue acts impulsively, telling a lie and starting a rumor. Blue's story-telling sets off a series of birds behaving badly.

As the news travels throughout the neighborhood birds, each reacts with a different, but typical, response. Green is nosy and a bit too excited about the possibility of drama. He assumes what Blue said was true and embellishes on the falsehood, not only repeating it, but also changing it into a more dramatic story. When told about the fight between friends, Violet, Orange, and Pink decide to fly along, hoping to witness the feud.

Red models positive problem-solving skills. When confronted with the gossip, Red works to remain calm. He chooses to solve the problem by being direct. Not only does he use his words assertively, but he also takes responsibility for unintentionally hurting Blue. Red is forgiving, even though Blue's words were untrue.

Helping Children Cope With Conflict

Conflict is a natural occurrence when we share our lives with others. When an offense happens, kids need to see it as an opportunity to be a problem solver. We can't always control the situation, but we are all responsible for our own feelings and how we choose to deal with them.

Remain calm. All feelings are acceptable, even foul ones. Help kids recognize when their mood shifts to an unwanted emotion. Simply reflect, "It looks like you are feeling…." Stay calm and reassure them that you believe they can work through the conflict. It's okay (even expected!) if a child has trouble with pausing and identifying their feelings at first. Be persistent in coaching them, and eventually they will start doing it on their own. This pause before action is key to being a productive problem solver. Perhaps Blue would have never lied if he was able to think before speaking.

Talk it out. When talking it out, focus on the feeling, not the person. For example, "I felt mad when she took the last cookie," instead of "I'm mad at her for taking the last cookie." Encourage your child to own the emotion. Emphasize that it is not the person who caused the feeling, it was their action. It is easier to forgive and move on when you speak to *what* triggered the hurt, not *who*. Help kids by reflecting on your own moods throughout the day. For example, "I was so embarrassed being late for my meeting." Explain the difference between what you are feeling and what occurred to make you feel that way: e.g. embarrassment vs. being late. Blue felt mad when he wasn't invited to go hunt for worms. His job was to deal with his feelings, not get back at Red for leaving him out.

Move on. The easiest way to end a conflict is to state how you feel and give the person who hurt you the opportunity to apologize. Most of the time, that's all that is needed, as long as you are willing to forgive the offense. In order to move on, everyone involved needs to take responsibility for their words and actions. Children are often defensive and may find it difficult to accept that what they did was hurtful. Responses like "But he made me mad!" or "It's not my fault" are typical. Again, focus on the action, not the person. "You chose to use your hands, we never solve problems that way." Or "Even if they used upsetting words, you need to use helpful ones." Kids aren't bad for making a mistakes—mistakes happen. Emphasize that there is no need to feel ashamed, as long as they do their best to make the situation better and learn to do better next time.

Teaching Life Skills

The colorful birds in the story get caught up in the drama of the moment. Their actions illustrate some fundamental truths that kids need in order to get along. Whether at home, at school, or any other social setting, it takes skill to be a cooperative member of a group.

Honesty is the best policy. Lying is a coping strategy, albeit not a good one. Blue told the first lie to feel better about what happened. That didn't work. Blue then told a second lie to cover up his first lie. That didn't work either. Developmentally, it is typical for kids to use falsehoods. Blue teaches us the importance of being honest with yourself and others. When you know your child is lying, be gentle

yet firm. Act on what you know is true; don't argue the point. If you belabor the act of lying, you may lose sight of the reason your child lied. Talk about the importance of trust and how they could have handled the situation better. If your child continues to insist they didn't lie, don't engage. As a parent, we talk to our kids all the time about all sorts of things. Let them know you are just teaching them something important. Their job as a child is to listen, yours is to teach. Stick to the fact that you are not talking about the lie, you are helping them learn how to handle situations in a positive way.

Don't believe everything you hear. It is sad but true: People love gossip. Stories spread from one person to the next, often changing along the way. Green chose to believe Blue's hurtful words and even changed them into a bigger lie, creating a dramatic whirlwind of events. Emphasize to kids that when they repeat hurtful things, they actually become part of the problem and can even make the situation worse. You can use the example of the birds in the story who just came to watch the fight; they probably didn't think they were making the situation worse, since as far as they knew, the fight was already happening. But in reality, their spreading of the story was the main source of drama! Even if a conversation about another seems harmless, it's a good standard of behavior to not talk about a person who is not there to give their side of the story. Teach children to stop gossip in its tracks. By saying, "I don't talk about other people," they then become an upstander and may be saving someone from hurt feelings.

Be kind. Kind actions bind friends together. Being nice not only makes other people feel good, it also makes you feel good about yourself. Kids can easily understand the theory of "what goes around, comes around." If you want others to treat you right, you must begin by doing the right thing yourself. By being forgiving and reflecting on his own mistake, Red models compassion and is able to set the situation to rights. Being kind in any situation will result in positive feelings all around.

About the Author

Lysa Mullady is the author of *Bye Bye Pesky Fly,* which was her first book. She has been an elementary school counselor for 29 years and is known for her engaging, enthusiastic, and creative counseling style. Her passion is to teach her students to be problem solvers by talking it out and thinking good things. Lysa was born and raised on Long Island, where she still lives with her family and two goldendoodles. You can find her on the weekends enjoying the beach with her husband, walking the dogs and searching for beach glass, all while imagining ways to help others become the best they can be.

About the Illustrator

Kyle Reed is an illustrator from Hamilton, Ontario, Canada. His digital and traditional collage work has appeared in children's books, magazines, animation, and advertising. Kyle has been bird watching once, and looks forward to going again.

About Magination Press

Magination Press is the children's book imprint of the American Psychological Association, the largest scientific and professional organization representing psychologists in the United States and the largest association of psychologists worldwide.